D1457162

FAMOUS FINISHES

FAMOUS FINISHES

Ann Graham Gaines

with additional text by Jeff Gluck

CHELSEA HOUSE
PUBLISHERS

A Haights Cross Communications Company ®

Philadelphia

Cover Photo: Ricky Craven (32) beats Kurt Busch by .002 seconds to win NASCAR's closest finish, Darlington Raceway, March 16, 2003.

CHELSEA HOUSE PUBLISHERS

VP, NEW PRODUCT DEVELOPMENT   Sally Cheney
DIRECTOR OF PRODUCTION   Kim Shinners
CREATIVE MANAGER   Takeshi Takahashi
MANUFACTURING MANAGER   Diann Grasse

STAFF FOR FAMOUS FINISHES
EDITORIAL ASSISTANT Sarah Sharpless
PRODUCTION EDITOR Bonnie Cohen
PHOTO EDITOR Pat Holl
SERIES DESIGN AND LAYOUT Hierophant Publishing Services/EON PreMedia

Original edition first published in 1999.

http://www.chelseahouse.com

A Haights Cross Communications ◀── Company ®

First Printing

1   3   5   7   9   8   6   4   2

Library of Congress Cataloging-in-Publication Data

Gaines, Ann.
   Famous finishes/Ann Graham Gaines with additional text by Jeff Gluck.
      p. cm.
   Includes bibliographical references and index.
   ISBN 0-7910-8758-1
   1. Automobile racing—History—Juvenile literature. I. Title.
GV1029.15.G35 2005
796.72—dc22

                                                                2005010395

All links and Web addresses were checked and verified to be correct at the time of publication. Because of the dynamic nature of the Web, some addresses and links may have changed since publication and may no longer be valid.

TABLE OF CONTENTS

NASCAR'S CLOSEST FINISH

Ricky Craven and Kurt Busch began bumping each other with three laps to go. They didn't stop until they crossed the finish line .002 seconds apart. It was the closest recorded finish in **NASCAR** history.

The date was March 16, 2003, and the place was Darlington Raceway in Darlington, South Carolina. The usual field of 43 drivers had gathered for the Carolina Dodge Dealers 400, and the fans attending the NASCAR **Nextel Cup** event (formerly known as Winston Cup) at Darlington were treated to a race they'll never forget.

Busch and Craven won't forget it either.

In 2004, Craven told the media:

"To me, it was the equivalent of growing up as a kid . . . and thinking back to Carlton Fisk's home run in the sixth game of the '75 World Series or playing basketball and getting the last shot, you know, with a few seconds to go, or football. It was the equivalent of those types of sports, you know, sporting events in my mind growing up, you know, Boston College, the Hail Mary that they somehow caught. And, so it's really cool to be a part of that."[1]

Busch was leading the race with three laps remaining until he saw Craven pull up beside him. Suddenly, Busch smacked his car into the wall. Craven slipped by, but only for a moment. Busch responded by pulling a **cross-over** move on Craven. A cross-over is a driving technique where one driver gets past another by pulling down to the inside of the track and zooming around the other car.

Busch took the lead for roughly half a lap, but Craven quickly caught up. Still, Busch led almost the entire last lap, until Craven pulled down to the inside of the track.

When interviewed in 2004, Craven said:

"The problem was that we are both way too narrow-minded and selfish and we can't help thinking about one thing, and neither one of us were willing to let up. . . . At that point I was about just positioning myself for one last chance and that's what we got coming off at Turn Four in the last lap."[2]

That set up one of the most exciting finishes NASCAR has ever seen. The two cars came to the finish line, bumping and rubbing at full speed. In the end, Craven edged in front of Busch as the cars crossed the line. The race ended in a cloud of smoke as the drivers collided.

"All right! What a finish!" yelled FOX TV commentator Darrell Waltrip, who was calling the race.[3]

"Have you ever . . . ?" FOX's Mike Joy began to ask Waltrip.

"No, I've never!" Waltrip replied. "That's one great race right there."

Craven wasn't sure whether he won the race. It was so close that even the winning driver didn't know which car came in first.

Kurt Busch, right, and Ricky Craven (32) collide after NASCAR's closest finish at Darlington Raceway on March 16, 2003.

"I have not seen a replay of the race and I'm going to be honest with you," he told the media after the race. "I would really like to confirm that we actually won."[4]

Busch said that, despite losing, he still feels like he won because the finish was so exciting. In 2004, he told the media:

"For us to finish second in such an epic battle really didn't feel like a second place finish. I gave everything that I had, and it was choreographed in such a fashion where Ricky

Craven gave everything he had in a way that it looked like the two of us were destined to produce something like this and nothing forever would cross our minds of doing anything like that."[5]

At the time, Busch was just beginning his NASCAR career, while Craven's was nearing its end. Craven was 36 years old, while Busch was 24. In 2004, Craven lost his job driving the Tide car, while Busch went on to win the NASCAR Nextel Cup that season.

But both drivers will always be linked together, thanks to that one day of great racing. Many fans and observers felt that the finish was made better by its happy ending. While Craven celebrated in victory lane, Busch

Ricky Craven gives thumbs up after winning the side-by-side duel with Kurt Busch.

interrupted the party to congratulate Craven. The two drivers smiled, laughed, and hugged.

"You know, he has earned my respect," Craven said. "He is a good guy, a great racer, and I look forward to racing with him . . . down the road."[6]

Busch said he never thought of fighting with Craven, as sometimes happens in NASCAR. When some drivers miss out on winning or their cars get wrecked, sometimes they get very mad. That anger can result in a fight. But Busch said he's just happy to be part of the race's legacy.

Kurt Busch, one of NASCAR's young stars, waits to begin practice during the summer of 2004.

When interviewed in 2004, Busch said:

"I've told that [race] story a few times, maybe if I get up to 2,000 times of telling the story, I will gain that 2,000th [of a] second behind the whole time. I think it really counts as a win in my mind and to be part of something that special for everybody that looks up to the record books, it will be 2,000th of a second, and maybe by the year 3000 I will be ahead."[7]

Craven had a different idea of how to tell the story.

"Yeah, that might work, you know, and if that might work for somebody that far down the road, they haven't seen the race and he certainly deserves that. But from my seat, I'm going to be telling the story a long time also and I'm still going to win by 2,000th of the second."[8]

DID YOU KNOW?

The 2005 Daytona 500

The Daytona 500 is known as "The Great American Race." And until 2005, it was always exactly 500 miles long.

Jeff Gordon won the Daytona 500 in 2005, but the race was actually 507.5 miles long. That's because NASCAR implemented a new system in 2004 to guarantee racing fans an exciting finish.

In the past, NASCAR races would sometimes finish "under caution," meaning the yellow caution flag was out, and race cars had to go slower—even at the finish line. Cautions are given because of accidents on the track.

But starting in 2004, NASCAR made a new "green-white-checkered" finish. It was racing's equivalent of overtime.

If there's a wreck on the track near the end of the race, NASCAR officials now clean up the accident and then wave the green flag (meaning "go!"), then the white flag (meaning "one lap left"), and then the checkered flag (meaning "the race is over").

The 2005 Daytona 500 was the first time NASCAR had used the green-white-checkered finish in racing's Super Bowl. Gordon certainly didn't seem to mind.

② TO RUN PAST SOUND

The "Big Bad Black Monster" first came to the United States in the belly of a huge jet transport plane. When the plane landed at Reno, Nevada, the monster was rolled down onto the airport runway. By late afternoon, it was on display under the bright lights and mirrors of the Peppermill Casino in downtown Reno. It was painted jet black. The slender body of the *Thrust SSC* Supersonic jet automobile was made of aluminum, titanium, and miles of carbon fiber. It was 56 feet long. It weighed more than 14,000 pounds. It was powered by two 110,000-horsepower Rolls Royce jet engines, the same jet engines used in British supersonic fighter planes today. A seat for a single rider was welded in the center between the two jet engines. A long, pointed spear stuck out from the front. In its gleaming black armor, the machine looked a lot like a jet car for a knight from the days of King Arthur. And like a knight of old, the *Thrust SSC* had come to the desert to answer a challenge.

The *Thrust SSC* did not come alone or unprepared for the struggle. The jet transport also unloaded more than 90 tons of backup equipment from its belly. There were a Jaguar Firechase sedan, two Supacat tractors, a Merlo telescopic-boom handler that could easily pick up the *Thrust SSC*, two

Richard Noble with *Thrust SSC* on the Black Rock Desert flats. Designed by Ron Ayers and driven by Air Force pilot Andy Greene, it was the first land vehicle to exceed the speed of sound.

Palouste air starters for the jet engines, and two vehicle trailers. But that was not all: there were satellite communications equipment, computers, offices, a kitchen, and enough food to feed the crew for a month. It was a lot of stuff.

The next morning, September 3, 1997, a long motorcade left Reno heading north. The parade of vehicles included the towed *Thrust SSC* car near the front, followed by cargo vans, crew buses, cars, pickups, and motor homes. One hundred miles later, the *Thrust SSC* and her crew arrived at Black Rock Desert. It is some of the flattest land on earth, and was perfect for racing the *Thrust SSC*.

Sir Malcolm Campbell stands with his race car, *Bluebird*, which broke the land-speed record of 276 miles per hour.

The *Thrust SSC* had come to defeat three foes in that beautiful desert. The first foe was the **land-speed record,** held by whoever reaches the fastest recorded speed in the world while driving an automobile over the ground. Sir Malcolm Campbell of Great Britain was the first man to drive more than 300 miles per hour (mph). He did it in 1935 in his car, *Bluebird*, which used a 12-cylinder, 2,500-horsepower Rolls Royce aircraft engine.

Sometime around 1950, people began to use either rocket or jet engines to power their automobiles, and the land-speed record soon increased. On October 23, 1970,

The Blue Flame in a trial run just before it set a new land-speed record on the Bonneville Salt Flats in 1970.

Gary Gabelich of the United States used a liquid natural gas–hydrogen peroxide rocket engine in his automobile, *The Blue Flame*, to achieve a land-speed record of 630.388 mph. Soon the problem was not going fast, but staying on the ground. When Stan Barrett drove the *Budweiser Rocket* across Edwards Air Force Base at more than 700 mph, the 100-pound solid wheels rose 10 inches off the ground.

The second foe of the *Thrust SSC* was the sound barrier. Fifty years before, Chuck Yeager of the United States had first traveled faster than the speed of sound in a

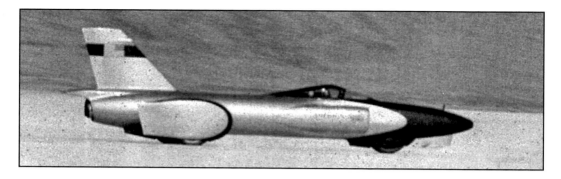

Land-speed record setter Craig Breedlove, streaks across the Utah salt flats in his jet powered *Spirit of America* at speeds greater than 468 miles per hour.

Bell X-1 rocket-powered airplane 37,000 feet above the desert sands of Nevada. As the nose of the plane passed through the **sound barrier**, a shock wave followed behind it. When that wave was heard, it sounded like an explosion. Other effects of the wave disappeared harmlessly around the airplane at the high altitude, but no one knew what would happen when that kind of shock wave was created and struck the ground only a few inches below the supersonic car. Someone would have to break the sound barrier to find out.

The third foe of the *Thrust SSC* was Craig Breedlove. He and Richard Noble, the owner of the *Thrust SSC*, had battled before. Now 60 years old, Breedlove was the first man ever to go 400, 500, and 600 mph on land. On October 4, 1983, on the same Black Rock Desert, Noble drove a Rolls Royce jet-powered car, *Thrust II*, to a timed two-way average speed of 633.468 mph. It took the land-speed record away from Breedlove. Both men were retired, but the flame of desire continued to burn in both of them. In 1990, Breedlove told Noble that he had acquired two GE J-79 turbojets and was planning another assault on the land-speed record, then held by Gary Gabelich.

Each immediately realized that the one who won the next land-speed record would probably also break the sound barrier in an automobile for the first time. It was a worthy challenge for these old warriors of speed.

Noble returned to England and built the *Thrust SSC*. Ron Ayers, the designer, decided to use twin jet engines up front with a long thin fuselage, and place the driver at the center between the jet engines. There were no **wind tunnels** that could test the stability of such a vehicle on a road at that speed. Noble and Ayers decided to use a **mainframe computer** for the engineering work. They added some new features to their vehicle. The car would be steered with the rear wheels to help keep it on the ground. The car was finished by the autumn of 1995, and the first tests were done during 1996.

Andy Green was chosen from 32 applicants to be the driver of the *Thrust SSC*. His professional job was piloting his Royal Air Force Tornado F3 fighter–bomber, which has a top speed of more than 1,500 mph. "There is no glory from taking risks," he says. "You can't do it well if you are excited, and you can't if you are so laid back you are half-asleep."

Ayers said of his driver, "Andy knows more about the car than all of us put together. He has the capability to feel exactly what is happening with the car."

Each side planned its assault on the record very carefully. When the *Thrust SSC* crews arrived, Breedlove was already set up and ready to go. They agreed that both cars would get a chance each day to run. They would flip a coin to see who would have the right to go first. It was agreed that an official land-speed record would be the average of two runs of the course within an hour. It was an exacting standard.

Craig Breedlove sits in the cockpit of his $3 million rocket-powered car at his *Spirit of America* headquarters in Rio Vista, California.

Each side had drawn up a plan to get their car ready. Any mistake would be a disaster. Both cars were equipped with computer systems that made human drivers almost unnecessary. The engineers in the pit crews ran the cars with a computer program they called a "run profile." The human driver made small steering changes and mostly hung on. In all, the *Thrust SSC* made 66 runs in the Nevada Desert, but only one or two were actual attempts at the record. Most runs tested the driving condition, the accuracy of the engineers' predictions, and the performance of the car's engine, tires, suspension, or computer system.

For example, at 7:30 in the morning on September 8, 1997, the *Thrust SSC* crews readied the computers and communications equipment. A quick, dull roar could be heard all over the vast desert floor as Andy Green barely pushed the car's throttle. It shot a long rooster tail of dust out behind as it raced to 148 mph in just a couple of seconds. Green immediately throttled back to idle and let the car roll to a complete stop 1.72 miles from the starting line. This was exactly where the engineers had predicted the car would stop. This successful run was a test not of the car, but of the slickness of the Black Rock Desert's surface dirt. Too slick, and the tires would not hold; too sticky, and it would take more power to push the jet to a new record. They had to know before trying for the record.

That same afternoon, Breedlove drove the *Spirit of America* on a one-way run of 348 mph in a successful test run of his own. But soon, problems halted both teams. The *Thrust SSC* team had a series of computer problems, and the *Spirit of America* swallowed a foreign object that destroyed its jet engine. The *Spirit of America* crew had to take the car back to California to switch to the spare jet engine.

Under a cloudless sky in the early morning of October 15, 1997, with very little breeze, Green recorded a run of 759.333 mph on the first run of the morning. With just barely seconds to spare, the crew turned the car around and readied it for its return trip. The speed for the second run was measured at more than 765 mph, faster than the speed of sound. Spectators heard a dull explosion as the sound barrier was broken, but everything was fine.

Marc Sampson, a member of Breedlove's team, followed the return trip in a light airplane. Sampson reported, "As *Thrust* worked up to speed, a huge dust trail followed it. Then, when it reached the sound barrier, the dust cloud rose off the ground and followed the car until it passed out of the sound barrier, and then the cloud returned to the ground. I do not know what it means, but it was unbelievable to see."

From the ground view, when the car broke the sound barrier, the shock wave was visible in front of and under the trailing dust cloud. The sound wave under the car erased its

Andy Green would probably laugh at race car drivers.

When Green traveled 765 mph in 1997 to set the land-speed record, it was an amazing feat that has not since been equaled.

As fast as NASCAR and Indy Racing League cars travel, they don't even come close to the Thrust SSC.

NASCAR Nextel Cup cars are among the slowest of the major motor sports vehicles. The stock cars can travel at speeds of more than 200 mph, but most races are driven in the upper 100s.

Cars that drive in the Indianapolis 500 are much smaller than those in the NASCAR Nextel Cup and have different engines. Speeds of up to 237 mph have been recorded during the Indy 500.

The fastest race cars drive in the National Hot Rod Association. NHRA cars travel only a short distance during each race in a format called drag racing. NHRA cars travel between 320 and 330 mph at full speed, although they do so for less than 5 seconds.

tire tracks. It was eerie. It looked as if the car left no earthly record of its time beyond the sound barrier.

The *Thrust SSC* had beaten all three foes. When asked what he thought the fastest *Thrust SSC* might go, Green nodded when someone mentioned, "850 mph?" "Certainly," he said. "Not out of the question," he replied when someone asked, "1000 mph?" "But a longer course would be needed. And there isn't one we know of." It was time to go home.

③ THE FIRST INDY 500

One of the most important automobile races in the world is the **Indianapolis 500**-mile race. It is held each year on Memorial Day at the "Brickyard," a 2.5-mile race track in Indianapolis, Indiana. On race day, more than 250,000 people fill the seats around the track, and millions more all over the world watch the race on television. The record speed around the track is more than 237 mph. In 2004, the prize money for the race totaled more than $10 million. The race track has changed only a little since it was constructed by Carl Fisher as a place to test new racing cars.

Fisher was a race car driver in the earliest days of the sport. In 1905, Fisher lost an important race in France and he was unhappy with his automobile. He said that cars from Europe could "go uphill faster than the American cars can come down." When Fisher returned to the United States, he decided to build a place where new American racing cars could be tested and improved. In 1909, he and some friends formed the Indianapolis Motor Speedway Company. They bought a 320-acre farm on the west side of town and changed it into a 2.5-mile, oval race track. The two, long straight parts of the oval are 3,300 feet long; the two, short straights are 660 feet long; the four turns are each 1,320 feet long. The track was made of crushed stone.

Smoke fills the air as the drivers start their engines at the Brickyard in 1909.

On August 19, 1909, the first race was held at the new track. It was a disaster. The speeding cars quickly tore up the track's surface, and two accidents occurred when drivers lost control of their cars at high speed. Four people, a driver, a mechanic, and two spectators, were killed before Fisher could stop the race.

Fisher had the crushed stone removed and the surface of the entire oval track paved with 3.2 million 10-pound bricks. Since then, the track has been known as the "Brickyard." Most of the original bricks remain as the foundation of the race track today. Some short races were held in 1910. Fisher then announced plans for the greatest race of all time, a 500-mile race to be completed in one day. The prize money

Henry Ford took this photo of the drivers lined up in front of their cars at the first Indy 500 in 1911.

for winning this "International Sweepstakes" was $14,000, a very large amount of money for that time.

On May 30, 1911, Memorial Day, 80,000 people attended the first 500-mile race. Forty cars from all over the United States entered. Each car was a giant of its day, each weighed at least 2,300 pounds, and each was powered by an engine that pushed the car along with power equivalent to 100 horses. The cars had big, wooden-spoke wheels and thin, knobby tires that frequently went flat. All of the cars except one carried two passengers, a driver, and a mechanic. They sat side-by-side in tiny leather-covered buckets high off the ground. The job of the mechanic was to pump the gasoline from the tank to the engine and to help change the tires if they went flat during the race. His most important job, however, was to look out behind the car and tell the driver about the oncoming cars.

These race cars had little to stop them because they only had brakes on the rear wheels. The cars were steered by huge, wooden, steering wheels that caused blisters on the drivers' hands because they shook so much due to the brick race track. The cars had no windshields, and all drivers wore goggles that quickly became spotted with the oil and grease that poured from the engines and soon covered the track. And even though these racing cars were primitive by today's standards, they were fast. On the straight parts of the track, these machines could reach almost 100 mph.

One of the racing cars that was lined up in the sixth of eight rows at the start was different from all of the rest. The Marmon Wasp was painted bright yellow and black, and was smaller and lower than the other cars. Its engine was not nearly as powerful as the other cars in the race, and the cockpit had only one seat for a single driver. The car was streamlined, shaped like a cone with the point to the rear. On top of the cone was a tail, like an airplane tail, to keep the car on line. Because there would be no mechanic to watch out behind, the car had a rear-view mirror mounted on top of the hood. The driver of the Wasp was a local man named Ray Harroun, who had designed and built the car himself.

To keep the race safe at the start, a passenger car led the racers around the track for a single lap so that they could get a running start at 40 mph. This was the first time a **pace car** was used in racing. To this day, each year the Indianapolis race is started with a pace car. More than 100 assistants were

Joe Jagersberger (8) driving a Case, flanked by Will Jones (9) also in a Case, and Louis Disbrow (5) in a Pope-Hartford, speed into the first turn on the Brickyard.

used to time and keep track of the cars during the race. A complicated timing system was used that recorded the time in hundredths of a second. As each car passed under the judging stand, it tripped a wire that was stretched across the track 1 foot from the ground. Fisher had made every effort to make the race safe and the judging accurate. But it was not to be.

On the very first lap of the race, the wire across the track broke and had to be repaired quickly. The race began as a duel between two of the larger two-seaters. David Bruce-Brown in a maroon Fiat and Ralph Mulford in a white Lozier passed

Spectators watch the first 500-mile Memorial Day race from inside the Brickyard oval.

each other for the lead on almost every one of the early laps in the scheduled 200-lap race. Harroun in the Marmon Wasp began the race near the back of the pack but made slow, steady progress toward the leaders as the race continued. He kept the Wasp at a comfortable 75 mph, and soon passed many of the bigger cars as they stopped to change tires or make repairs.

Nearly halfway through the race, at about the 240-mile mark, Joe Jagersberger in a Case racer lost control of his car when the steering wheel broke. With nothing to steer it, the car veered wildly back and forth across the track. Finally, the car crashed into the judging stand, just as the judges jumped to the ground to safety. The unguided car then went down pit row, threw the riding mechanic out onto the ground, and continued down the track to finally stop in the infield.

Harry Knight in a Westcott was the next car on the scene. Knight swerved to avoid hitting the mechanic lying on the track. He crashed into pit row and hit the parked Apperson car of Herbert Lytle. Knight's riding mechanic was also thrown onto the track. He suffered the only injury of the entire series of accidents, a bruised back from which he later fully recovered. By now, the track was filled with wrecked cars, smashed lumber from the judging stand, and at least two people lying in harm's way. The next two cars to pass the scene were the leaders of the race, Mulford in his Lozier and Bruce-Brown in his Fiat. Somehow, Mulford steered his car through all of the obstacles, followed closely by Bruce-Brown and the other cars coming from behind.

The track was soon cleared, but none of the judges were keeping track of the cars and their places in the race. Most of the judges were on the track giving advice and helping to clear the debris. There was no one to count the laps as the cars passed the judging stand, and no one was sure of who was winning.

Most of the time during this huge accident, the Marmon Wasp was in pit row, changing drivers. No one noticed when Harroun pulled out of pit row. Was he in front of or behind the two leaders, Mulford and Bruce-Brown? Were they all on the same lap? The *Indianapolis News* reported the next morning that Harroun took over the lead at the 200-mile mark of the race, before the accident. The official and final results of the judges said that the Wasp did not take the lead until the 257-mile mark, after the accident. No one knew for sure how many laps each car had run, but the race continued anyway. No other serious accidents occurred, and the three leaders were in a duel, lap after lap, as the close race continued. When the judges, now back in the judging stand, waved the green flag to signal that there was only one lap to go, Mulford, Bruce-Brown, and Harroun flew by, in that order.

On the very last lap, Bruce-Brown's Fiat broke a spark lever and coasted to a stop. Mulford's Lozier crossed the finish line first, closely followed by the Wasp. The judges

Ray Harroun won the first Indianapolis 500 in 1911 in Number 32, a Marmon Wasp.

were still not sure who had won. Was Mulford the winner, or was he a lap or two behind Harroun? The judges waved Mulford on, making him take another couple of laps. Harroun simply pulled the Wasp over to the side of the course and stopped. Each side claimed victory. The judges announced that no decision would be made immediately, and that they would announce the winner the next morning.

The Lozier team claimed they had won. The judges' very own scoreboard had Mulford in first place. But, they soon claimed that their own scorekeeping at the judging stand was wrong because of the confusion caused by the

Ray Harroun, winner of the 1911 Indy 500, in his racing helmet and goggles.

accidents. Another 100 judges were positioned around the course and had not been involved in the accidents near pit row. One of them claimed that Mulford had had the lead until lap 181 when the Wasp took over first spot and kept it to the end of the race. Newspaper accounts of the race claimed that the Wasp had taken the lead at lap 100 before the accidents at the judges' stand, and had never given it up. It was also learned that the timing wire had broken a second time and that it had taken more than an hour to fix it during the course of the race. It was a mess.

The next morning, the "official" results were announced. Harroun was declared the winner with a time of 6:41:08, Mulford was second with a time of 6:46:46, and Bruce-Brown was third with a time of 6:52:29. As soon as this news was announced, protests were filed. Bruce-Brown insisted that he had finished second, a lap ahead of Mulford. No one was satisfied, and more protests were made. The judges met again and "official" results were posted for a second time. The top three finishers had not changed, but their times had. Harroun lost a full minute, and his time was listed at 6:42:08. Mulford gained about three minutes at 6:43:51. Bruce-Brown's time remained the same.

Changes were also made to the other finishers in the race. Joe Dawson, in another Marmon, was given credit for a lap no one recorded. He then was placed fifth, bumping everybody else down one finishing position. The final places

DID YOU KNOW?

Famous Fishers

Carl Fisher, the founder of the Indianapolis 500, isn't the only famous Fisher associated with the race.

At age 19, Sarah Fisher (no relation to Carl) became the third woman ever to race in the Indy 500. She was also one of the youngest.

Sarah Fisher raced in the Indy 500 five times as of early 2005, recording finishes as high as 21st.

With the rise of NASCAR, however, interest in cars that run in the Indianapolis 500 has suffered. Sarah Fisher realized that and started a new career in the low ranks of NASCAR in 2005.

But while she was driving Indy cars, Sarah Fisher was loved by racing fans. She was named the Indy Racing League's most popular driver three times.

The original Marmon Wasp is on display at the Indianapolis
Motor Speedway Hall of Fame Museum, Indianapolis, Indiana.

of Fred Belcher's Knox racer and Harry Cobe's Jackson
automobile were switched, finally ending up ninth and tenth.
After the final meeting of the judges, all of the lap records for
the race cars were destroyed. The only record found in later
years in the confidential records of the Indianapolis 500 is a
handwritten note that reads, "Mechanical devices for scoring
should be avoided at major contests. They can break down
and at best are only as good as the operator."

Harroun took the first-place prize money and placed his
name in the record books as the winner of the first Indianapolis
500. Many doubts remain about what really happened in that
exciting race. There was no doubt in the minds of the spectators, however. It was a spectacular, exciting race, regardless
of who won. The next year, the race was held again in front of
an even bigger crowd. Every year since then, the crowd gets
bigger, the race cars go faster, and the prize money increases
when the fastest cars in the world meet at the "Brickyard."

MAYFIELD BUMPS "THE INTIMIDATOR"

Jeremy Mayfield is probably still looking over his shoulder. As a young, up-and-coming NASCAR Nextel Cup Series driver in June 2000, Mayfield was racing as hard as he could during the **Pocono 500** at the Pocono Raceway in Pennsylvania.

But to win the race, he had to pull off something that many other drivers wouldn't dare to try: bump Dale Earnhardt Sr., the famous "Intimidator."

Earnhardt had made his career off his rough style, not giving an inch on the track and using his car to move other competitors out of his way. The methods worked, to be sure. Earnhardt won seven Nextel Cup championships in his storied career.

But at Pocono, Mayfield tried to put all that out of his mind. With just two career victories entering the race, Mayfield wanted to take advantage of being near the front of the pack. And he didn't want to make a mistake that would cost him the race.

In 2004, Mayfield recalled: "Throughout that day at Pocono we were back and forth, whether it was first and second, third and fourth. It seemed like we were in the top five all day racing each other. He would drive behind me and

Dale Earnhardt Sr., "The Intimidator," was known for using his car to move others out of his way.

get me loose, and I would move out of the way. A few minutes later we'd get him back, and we did that all day long."[9]

Mayfield and Earnhardt pitted at the same time, with roughly 30 laps to go. Each driver took two tires and left **pit road**, ready to duel to the most memorable finish of Mayfield's career.

"(The pit stop) put him first and me second," Mayfield said. "I knew then if I try anything between now and the end of the race to pass him, if I do get in front of him, he's going to probably turn me or get me loose, and I'm going to lose the race."[10]

Earnhardt had made his reputation pulling moves like that. But no one expected Mayfield would beat "The Intimidator" at his own game.

Jeremy Mayfield (12) passes Dale Earnhardt Sr. (3) to win the 2000 Pocono 500.

With five laps to go, Mayfield was right on Earnhardt's back bumper. He knew there would only be one chance, one shot to pass Earnhardt's No. 3 GM Goodwrench car.

Mayfield waited until the last lap. Coming out of the third and final turn of Pocono's triangular track, Mayfield prepared to knock Earnhardt's car. Whether or not the two cars actually touched is still in question, but a phenomenon called "**aero-loose**" created a bump. Race cars travel so fast that they create an air flow over the vehicle. When another car gets close enough to disrupt the air near the car's back end, the driver may sometimes experience a "loose" feeling. That means the back end becomes harder to control.

When Mayfield dipped the **nose** of his car under Earnhardt's, the No. 3 car wiggled and allowed Mayfield

Jeremy Mayfield's crew celebrates their victory over "The Intimidator" at the Pocono 500.

to scoot around "The Intimidator" and streak to the finish line.

Earnhardt was forced to save his car from crashing into the wall. In one turn, he had gone from first to fourth.

"This was for all the guys who have endured beatings by the school yard bully," sports writer Bill Fleischman wrote in the next day's *Philadelphia Daily News*. "This was the bold youngster who took down the sinister gunslinger."[11]

Mayfield proclaimed after the race that he wasn't scared of Earnhardt and he was trying to "rattle his cage." But behind the scenes, Mayfield stayed away from "The Intimidator" for the next 2 weeks.

In June 2004, Mayfield said: "I avoided him, . . . and I'm sure you know why. Next time I saw him and he grabbed me and gave me a knuckle on my head a little bit and joked with me. I said to him, 'Man, I thought you were going to be mad at me.' He said, 'Nah I'm not mad; I'm mad at a couple things you said.'"[12]

Jeremy Mayfield became the last driver to qualify for NASCAR's "Chase for the Nextel Cup" in 2004.

The Chase was a new way to decide the champion of the NASCAR season. Before, race car drivers earned season points that would determine the champion after the entire 36-race season.

Starting with the 2004 season, that changed. NASCAR decided that it needed a playoff system to make more fans interested in the sport.

After the first 26 races, only the top 10 drivers are eligible for the Chase, which is 10 weeks long. The other drivers still race in all the events, but they can't win the Nextel Cup.

The Chase means that even the 10th-place driver can win the championship. In the past, only two or three drivers would still have a chance to get the Nextel Cup with 10 races left.

But more fans—like the ones that follow Mayfield—can now be interested in the season's final 10 weeks.

Before Earnhardt walked away, Mayfield had just one question for one of the best, most-feared drivers in NASCAR history.

"If you were me and you bumped Dale Earnhardt at the last corner of the last lap at Pocono to win the race, and you won," Mayfield asked Earnhardt, "what would you do?"

Recalled Mayfield, "He smiled big and walked off."[13]

Mayfield went on to have a lackluster season, finishing 24th in the Nextel Cup standings. Earnhardt didn't miss his eighth championship by much, ending the season in second place.

The paths of Mayfield and Earnhardt never met again after that day in June. Seven months later, racing in the 2001 Daytona 500, Earnhardt was killed on the last lap of the race.

As much as some fans and drivers liked to see Earnhardt lose, "The Intimidator's" death was a crushing blow to racing.

"He was just an awesome guy, and he could dish it out and he could take it also," Mayfield said. "I think it's a sign of a true champion."[14]

The Pocono 500 was Mayfield's career highlight until a September night in 2004 at Richmond International Raceway. NASCAR introduced a new points system earlier that season, where the top 10 drivers would participate in a playoff-style format.

Mayfield was desperate to get into the top 10, but the only way to do it was to win. And that's exactly what he did.

When Mayfield retires, winning at Richmond might be his favorite memory. But it's unlikely he'll never be involved in a more famous finish than that June day at Pocono, where he bumped "The Intimidator" to win the race.

5

END OF AN ERA

Auto racing developed differently in Europe and the United States. Races in Europe were usually conducted on the regular highways of the countryside and were called **road races**. When closed loops of the highways were used to make a race course, they naturally had turns in every direction as well as being up and down hills or mountains. These loops became famous European courses with names like Nurburgring and Monza. They included such famous obstacles as narrow bridges, blind turns, tunnels, and city streets. These races often tested the driver's skill at changing gears as much as they tested the power and steering of the cars.

Naturally, the race cars of Europe and the United States developed differently because of the demands of the different kinds of racing. Beginning with the same basic design of a "horseless carriage," racing cars on the two continents evolved into very different machines. European cars became light and nimble; they had great steering control, huge brakes, and strong, finely tuned suspension systems to keep them under control at all times, and at all speeds. The engines were lightweight with only moderate power, but they were coupled to strong four- and five-speed transmissions that allowed instant power through all the gears. By the 1960s, European race car engines were mounted behind the driver, who was placed close to the ground and in front where visibility was the best. At that time, the typical European race car was mounted with a 4-cylinder, 2.5-liter, 175-horsepower engine.

Race cars in the United States were built on the concept of power first, because they raced on oval tracks. They only had to go fast: no left and right turns, and few gear changes. To go fast, they needed power. The cars were built big and heavy. They didn't steer well or even brake well, but they were quick. They used an engine that was so powerful that on the oval of the "Brickyard," it didn't matter how much the car weighed or how poorly it handled.

By far, the most popular and successful American racing engine manufacturer was the Offenhauser Company. Thirteen years in a row, an Offenhauser engine powered the winner of the Indianapolis 500 race. In the 1960s, the state-of-the-art Offenhauser engine was a 4.2-liter, 4-cylinder monster that produced more than 400 horsepower. The roadsters they powered looked like a typical sports car today: the driver was seated toward the rear and looked out over the hood of the engine in front of him. The entire appearance of the car was more substantial: bigger, heavier, and more durable than the European cars.

For almost half a century, these two styles of racing cars developed apart. European racing teams thought the Indy race was not worth contesting because of the premium placed on raw speed. However, in 1961, John Cooper and Jack Brabham were invited to bring a European car to the Indianapolis 500. They brought a specially modified Cooper Formula One road racer with them from England.

American and European drivers had little love for each other. Racers are a brash lot, known for speaking their minds

Jack Brabham drove the Cooper-Climax, a specially modified
Formula One road racer, at the 1961 Indianapolis 500.

to anyone who will listen. A.J. Foyt called the European car a
"bunch of tubes held together with chicken wire," and loudly
stated he would never drive one. Jim Clark declared, when
asked about the Indianapolis 500 race, "Imagine being paid
that amount of money for turning left 800 times."

Brabham quickly learned the course and posted a respectable qualifying run for the race. In the 1961 race, Brabham
finished ninth. The European car could corner much faster
than the best of the roadsters, and it was nearly as fast. But
the high-speed tires of the American cars were much more
durable than European Grand Prix tires, and Brabham was

forced to make twice as many stops for new tires as the Americans. Brabham's more than respectable finish in the race made other Grand Prix manufacturers in Europe decide to try their luck.

In July 1962, Colin Chapman and Dan Gurney made a deal with the Ford Motor Company to power their Lotus Formula One car in an attempt to win the Indianapolis 500 the next year. Ford developed a lightweight version of the Ford Fairlane V8 engine for their new Lotus 29. The new car and engine were tested and tuned on a private test track in Kingman, Arizona. Chapman liked the team's chances to win.

The Ford engine developed 80 horsepower less than the Offenhauser monsters, but the Lotus weighed nearly 500 pounds less than the American cars. The European car's superior cornering ability also increased its chances of a win. The greatest advantage of the new Lotus–Ford was that the engine ran on gasoline, a more economical fuel than the alcohol that was burned in the Offenhauser cars. The Lotus required two fewer pit stops than the bigger American cars. The Lotus crew appeared at Indianapolis for qualifying with three race-ready cars: one for Clark, one for Gurney, and a spare.

Parnelli Jones was favored to win the race. His car was the Agajanian Battery Special Watson–Offenhauser roadster, No. 98. The car was nicknamed *Ol' Calhoun*. Parnelli pushed *Ol' Calhoun* to a three-lap average of more than 151 to take the **pole position**. The next two fastest qualifiers also drove big "Offy" roadsters. At the start, all big American roadsters were in the front row. Clark qualified fast enough to be placed in the second row. He was completely surrounded by the big cars. Clark noted that it was "nothing but dust, smoke, and these giant cars around me. It was unreal."

Jim Clark in the Ford-powered Lotus. The Lotus weighed 500 pounds less than the Offenhauser cars and ran on gasoline.

At the start, Jones quickly took the lead and continued a record pace, breaking one lap record after another until lap 64 when he stopped for a routine pit stop. This allowed the Lotus–Ford to make up a lot of time. By lap 80, the European cars were in first and second place in the race. Jones was in third place and closing in on the leaders at a half-second a lap. Jones was going faster, but he had to stop more often. On lap 92, Jones passed Gurney as he retired into the pits. On lap 95, Clark pitted his car and Jones pulled into the lead.

Over the next 50 laps, *Ol' Calhoun* raced on. It opened a 40-second lead, but Clark's little, green Lotus stayed close behind, waiting. After both cars had completed their last pit stops, there were about 150 miles to go. Clark started cutting into Jones's lead with every lap. Clark **slipstreamed** the larger cars in front of him and then slipped by them in the turns. He skillfully wove between the cars on the track. In 30 laps, Clark cut Jones's lead from more than 40 seconds to 4. Clark later said, rather modestly, "Driving round Indianapolis is reasonably straightforward. I would go up through the gears but once in top I'd leave it in top and then give the brakes a dab coming into the corners. The big difficulty was judging the braking points, or the apex of a corner, as the track is quite featureless."

Just as the little Lotus pulled within view of the back of Jones's car, the oil tank mounted behind the driver in *Ol' Calhoun* split open. A stream of greasy smoke and dripping oil soon followed along behind Jones's car as it sped around the track. The oil made the track very slippery. Several cars lost control on the slippery parts of the track, spun out, and hit the walls.

Usually, a car that poses a danger such as this to the rest of the racers is "black-flagged," and forced to retire from the course. Chapman rushed up to the Clerk of the Course, Harlan Fengler, and demanded that Jones be black-flagged. Earlier in the race, the Novi V8 driven by Jim Hurtubise was flagged off the track for the same reason. Clark, in second place, slowed down, expecting the race officials to disqualify Jones and ensure Clark an easy victory. J.C. Agajanian, the sponsor of Jones's car, argued to Fengler that Jones should be allowed to continue. For some reason, Fengler put away the black flag, and allowed the race to continue under the yellow caution flag. Under a yellow-flag condition, cars must hold their positions on the course. It was just what the American car needed to win. Jones coasted to an easy victory.

Parnelli Jones in the Agajanian Battery Special Watson Offenhauser roadster, Number 98 nicknamed *Ol' Calhoun*.

Many in the crowd were outraged and cheered the little, green Lotus as the winner when it crossed the finish line some 30 seconds behind Jones's car. Jones and Agajanian argued to irate fans and other teams that their car had leaked no more oil than others. Most everyone else disagreed, rather loudly. When Eddie Sachs, one of the drivers who had crashed because of the slippery conditions, accused Jones of being a liar, Jones punched Sachs in the nose.

The big American roadsters may have won the battle that day, but they lost the war. The next year at Indianapolis, of the 61 cars entered, 21 were rear-engine cars, and 7 of the 10 fastest were rear-engine cars. Jones had a European-style road racer as a backup car. The Lotus team was forced to

Jim Clark smiles from the cockpit of his Lotus-Ford after setting a record qualifying speed of 158.8 miles per hour to win pole position for the 1964 Indy 500.

withdraw from the race because of tire trouble. The next year, however, Clark led the 1965 Indianapolis 500 from start to finish. His new Lotus 38 was powered by a 4-camshaft Ford V8 that developed 485 horsepower. Clark beat Jones, who was driving the Agajanian–Hurst Lotus–Ford, a European-style road racer almost identical to Clark's winning car. Clark won by almost two laps on the Indy oval, 1 minute, 58.97 seconds ahead of Jones. His average speed was more than 150 mph. The last foreign winner at Indianapolis had been Dario Resta driving a Peugeot in 1916.

Auto racing changes all the time. Every year the race cars get sleeker, faster, and better. The last big American-style roadster appeared in the 1966 Indy race. It was in the last row at the start. It looked old-fashioned and fat beside the other **aerodynamic** road racers. The changes in auto racing do not always come as quickly as they did at Indianapolis in 1963, but they always seem to come, a little bit at a time. Over a long period of time, the changes seem enormous. Race cars today are not horseless carriages; they are spaceships on wheels. But despite the changes in auto racing, fans will always be on hand to watch the best drivers in the world compete in the newest and hottest cars, and will be guaranteed the thrill of an exciting finish.

DID YOU KNOW?

Racing's popularity

The best place to see American-made race cars today is in NASCAR. And NASCAR's popularity has never been higher.

Today, the success of a sport is measured in television ratings. The 2005 Daytona 500 showed that NASCAR is indeed successful.

Television ratings are measured by the Nielsen Company. Nielsen uses electronic boxes in selected households to determine how many people are watching a certain show.

According to FOX Sports, which broadcasts NASCAR races, the last five Daytona 500s have had higher average TV ratings than the NBA Finals, The Masters Golf Tournament final rounds, and the Kentucky Derby horse races.

Even though the Daytona 500 is an afternoon race, it would have ranked* in the top 10 primetime shows for the week.

Clearly, auto racing is on the right track.

*FOXSports.com posting, February 23, 2005.

NOTES

Chapter 1

1. NASCAR media teleconference transcript; March 16, 2004.

2. Ibid.

3. NASCAR.com archived video of race.

4. GM Racing Notes and Quotes following Darlington Race.

5. NASCAR media teleconference; March 16, 2004.

6. Ibid.

7. Ibid.

8. Ibid.

Chapter 4

9. NASCAR media teleconference; June 8, 2004.

10. Ibid.

11. *Philadelphia Daily News*; June 19, 2000.

12. NASCAR media teleconference; June 8, 2004.

13. Ibid.

14. Ibid.

CHRONOLOGY

1894 First automobile race from Paris to Rouen, France, 90 miles.

1895 First automobile race in the United States from Chicago to Waukegan, Illinois.

1896 First oval track race in United States won at average speed of 26.8 mph.

1900 First closed-circuit race in Melun, France.

1904 Vanderbilt Cup Race starts road racing in America over 28-mile course in New York; land-speed record set at 103.6 mph in France.

1911 May 30: 80,000 people attend the first 500-mile race at Indianapolis Motor Speedway. Forty cars from all over the United States enter. Ray Harroun wins at average speed of 74.59 mph.

1927 Land-speed record set at 203.8 mph by Malcolm Campbell of Great Britain.

1935 Land-speed record set at 301.1 mph by Malcolm Campbell of Great Britain.

1947 Bill France Sr. organizes the National Association for Stock Car Auto Racing (NASCAR) in Daytona Beach, Florida.

1949 The first NASCAR champion, Red Byron, is crowned.

1950 Formula One Grand Prix Circuit races begin in Europe.

1957 August: Juan Fangio wins exciting race at Nurburgring, Germany, to ensure his fifth World Driving Championship title in Formula One Racing.

1959 Lee Petty wins 10 races in a Plymouth, including the first Daytona 500, to earn $45,570 on the NASCAR stock car racing circuit in the United States.

1963 May 30: Jim Clark drives first European road racer to a close and disputed second-place finish in the Indy 500 to mark the end of alcohol-burning American racers. Parnelli Jones wins the race at an average speed of 143.14 mph; land-speed record set at 407.4 mph by Craig Breedlove of the United States.

1964 Land-speed record set at 526.3 mph by Craig Breedlove of the United States.

1965 Land-speed record set at 600.6 mph by Craig Breedlove of the United States.

1967 Richard Petty wins 27 NASCAR races, including 10 in a row, en route to his second championship. It is the best season in NASCAR history.

1972 Winston becomes NASCAR's premier series title sponsor.

1979 Richard Petty wins his seventh Winston Cup championship.

1983 Land-speed record set at 633.5 mph by Richard Noble of Great Britain.

1984 Ronald Reagan becomes the first United States president to witness a NASCAR race.

1987 100,000 spectators line the race course at Silverstone, England, to see native son Nigel Mansell beat archrival Nelson Piquet.

1990 Arie Luyendyk of the Netherlands wins the Indianapolis 500 race with an average speed of 185.98 mph.

1994 Dale Earnhardt Sr., driving a Chevrolet, wins four races and his seventh NASCAR championship to earn $3,300,733.

1995 Jeff Gordon wins his first NASCAR Nextel Cup.

1997 October 15: Andy Green becomes first man to break the sound barrier in a wheeled vehicle with a run measured at more than 763.0 mph on the desert sands of Black Rock, Nevada.

2001 February 18: Dale Earnhardt Sr., a seven time NASCAR champion, is killed on the last lap of the Daytona 500 at age 49. Jeff Gordon wins his fourth NASCAR Cup championship.

2004 NASCAR switches its title series sponsors from Winston to Nextel. The Chase for the Nextel Cup is introduced. Dale Earnhardt Jr. wins the Daytona 500.

STATISTICS

Indianapolis 500 Winners

1911	Ray Harroun	1933	Louis Meyer
1912	Joe Dawson	1934	Bill Cummings
1913	Jules Goux	1935	Kelly Petillo
1914	Rene Thomas	1936	Louis Meyer
1915	Ralph DePalma	1937	Wilbur Shaw
1916	Dario Resta	1938	Floyd Roberts
1917–18	No race	1939	Wilbur Shaw
1919	Howard Wilcox	1940	Wilbur Shaw
1920	Gaston Chevrolet	1941	Floyd Davis, Mauri Rose
1921	Tommy Milton		
1922	Jimmy Murphy	1942–45	No race
1923	Tommy Milton	1946	George Robson
1924	L.L. Corum, Joe Boyer	1947	Mauri Rose
		1948	Mauri Rose
1925	Peter DePaolo	1949	Bill Holland
1926	Frank Lockhart	1950	Johnnie Parsons
1927	George Souders	1951	Lee Wallard
1928	Louis Meyer	1952	Troy Ruttman
1929	Ray Keech	1953	Bill Vukovich
1930	Billy Arnold	1954	Bill Vukovich
1931	Louis Schneider	1955	Bob Sweikert
1932	Fred Frame	1956	Pat Flaherty

1957	Sam Hanks	**1981**	Bobby Unser
1958	Jim Bryan	**1982**	Gordon Johncock
1959	Rodger Ward	**1983**	Tom Sneva
1960	Jim Rathmann	**1984**	Rick Mears
1961	A.J. Foyt	**1985**	Danny Sullivan
1962	Rodger Ward	**1986**	Bobby Rahal
1963	Parnelli Jones	**1987**	Al Unser
1964	A.J. Foyt	**1988**	Rick Mears
1965	Jim Clark	**1989**	Emerson Fittipaldi
1966	Graham Hill	**1990**	Arie Luyendyk
1967	A.J. Foyt	**1991**	Rick Mears
1968	Bobby Unser	**1992**	Al Unser Jr.
1969	Mario Andretti	**1993**	Emerson Fittipaldi
1970	Al Unser	**1994**	Al Unser Jr.
1971	Al Unser	**1995**	Jacques Villeneuve
1972	Mark Donohue	**1996**	Buddy Lazier
1973	Gordon Johncock	**1997**	Arie Luyendyk
1974	Johnny Rutherford	**1998**	Eddie Cheever
1975	Bobby Unser	**1999**	Kenny Brack
1976	Johnny Rutherford	**2000**	Juan Montoya
1977	A.J. Foyt	**2001**	Helio Castroneves
1978	Al Unser	**2002**	Helio Castroneves
1979	Rick Mears	**2003**	Gil de Ferran
1980	Johnny Rutherford	**2004**	Buddy Rice

NASCAR Nextel Cup Champions

1949	Red Byron	**1972**	Richard Petty
1950	Bill Rexford	**1973**	Benny Parsons
1951	Herb Thomas	**1974**	Richard Petty
1952	Tim Flock	**1975**	Richard Petty
1953	Herb Thomas	**1976**	Cale Yarborough
1954	Lee Petty	**1977**	Cale Yarborough
1955	Tim Flock	**1978**	Cale Yarborough
1956	Buck Baker	**1979**	Richard Petty
1957	Buck Baker	**1980**	Dale Earnhardt Sr.
1958	Lee Petty	**1981**	Darrell Waltrip
1959	Lee Petty	**1982**	Darrell Waltrip
1960	Rex White	**1983**	Bobby Allison
1961	Ned Jarrett	**1984**	Terry Labonte
1962	Joe Weatherly	**1985**	Darrell Waltrip
1963	Joe Weatherly	**1986**	Dale Earnhardt Sr.
1964	Richard Petty	**1987**	Dale Earnhardt Sr.
1965	Ned Jarrett	**1988**	Bill Elliott
1966	David Pearson	**1989**	Rusty Wallace
1967	Richard Petty	**1990**	Dale Earnhardt Sr.
1968	David Pearson	**1991**	Dale Earnhardt Sr.
1969	David Pearson	**1992**	Alan Kulwicki
1970	Bobby Isaac	**1993**	Dale Earnhardt Sr.
1971	Richard Petty	**1994**	Dale Earnhardt Sr.

1995	Jeff Gordon	**2000**	Bobby Labonte
1996	Terry Labonte	**2001**	Jeff Gordon
1997	Jeff Gordon	**2002**	Tony Stewart
1998	Jeff Gordon	**2003**	Matt Kenseth
1999	Dale Jarrett	**2004**	Kurt Busch

GLOSSARY

Aerodynamic: A shape designed specially to move faster through the air. Aerodynamic cars are smoother and flatter to avoid being slowed down by wind resistance.

Aero-loose: When the back of a race car loses its air because another car is close behind. This makes the back of the car slip or wiggle, which makes it harder to control.

Cross-over: A driving technique where one driver gets past another by pulling down to the inside of the track and zooming around the other car.

Indianapolis 500:   One of the world's most famous and historic races, the Indianapolis 500 is run every year by open-wheel style IndyCars at the Indianapolis Motor Speedway. The speedway holds more than 250,000 spectators, making it the largest sporting venue in the United States.

Land-speed record: The fastest a vehicle has ever moved across the ground.

Mainframe computer: Personal computers (PCs) don't always do the job, so big companies sometimes employ "mainframe computers," which are like pumped-up PCs. Mainframes were the early form of computers, before PCs were available to buy for the home and office. Personal computers cannot process information nearly as fast as mainframes can.

NASCAR: The National Association for Stock Car Auto Racing; the United States's premier auto racing organization. The NASCAR Nextel Cup is the second-most watched sport in the country behind NFL football.

Nextel Cup: NASCAR's premier racing level. NASCAR sanctions races on several levels, somewhat equivalent to minor league baseball. The Nextel Cup (formerly known as the Winston Cup) is like the major leagues.

Nose: The front of a race car, from the hood to the fender.

Pace car: Race cars don't always go full speed. During caution periods, cars need to follow a slower car in order to keep all the drivers together. This "pace car," driven by a race official, moves in front of the leader, and all the race cars must keep pace.

Pit Road: The off-track road where cars come down for brief servicing. During the race, pit crews change tires, add fuel and adjust race cars in brief periods called pit stops. The "pit" is where the crew waits for the car to stop for servicing.

Pocono 500: A NASCAR Nextel Cup race held at the Pocono Raceway in the Pennsylvania mountains. Most NASCAR races are named after the location of the track or a company that buys the rights to name the race whatever it wants.

Pole position: Race cars qualify to get into an event based on speed. The number one spot in the race is called the "pole position." The pole winner gets to start the race on the inside of the front row—the best place to be!

Road races: Instead of racing on ovals, race cars used to drive on actual roads and highways. Some racing organizations still hold races on actual roads, but most "road courses" today are on race tracks built with curves to simulate actual roads.

Slipstreamed: Race cars move so quickly that the air flows over them in a tight stream. When another car gets close behind, the air creates a suction that pulls the second car closer to the first one, increasing the speed of both. This is also known as "drafting."

Sound barrier: When a vehicle or aircraft goes so fast, it travels faster than sound can travel. This creates a break called a sonic boom, releasing a shock wave of sound.

Wind tunnel: A place to test a car's aerodynamic capability. A powerful engine shoots air at a vehicle, and engineers can see how the air flows over and around the car.

FURTHER READING

Buckley, James. *NASCAR: Speedway Superstars*. Reader's Digest Children's Publishing, 2004.

Canfield, Jack, et al. *Chicken Soup for the NASCAR Soul*. HCI, 2003.

Fresina, Michael J., ed. *Thunder and Glory: The 25 Most Memorable Races in NASCAR Winston Cup History*. Triumph Books, 2004

Garrow, Mark. *Dale Earnhardt: The Pass in the Grass and Other Incredible Moments from Racing's Greatest Legend*. Sports Publishing, 2001.

Guinness World Records 2005. Bantam, 2005.

Hembree, Mike. *Dale Earnhardt Jr.: Out of the Shadow of Greatness*. Sports Publishing, 2003.

Pimm, Nancy Roe. *Indy 500: The Inside Track*. Darby Creek Publishing, 2004.

Richard, Jon. *Fantastic Cutaway: Speed*. Copper Beech, 1997.

Stewart, Mark. *Auto Racing: A History of Cars and Fearless Drivers*. Franklin Watts, 1999.

Woods, Bob. *NASCAR: The Greatest Races*. Reader's Digest, 2004.

BIBLIOGRAPHY

Busch, Kurt. Interview by NASCAR media teleconference, March 16, 2004.

Craven, Ricky. Interview by NASCAR media tele-conference, March 16, 2004.

Craven, Ricky. Interview by GM Media Relations, March 16, 2003.

Fleischman, Bill. "Mayfield takes on Earnhardt, comes out on top." *Philadelphia Daily News*, June 19, 2000.

FOX TV broadcast, March 16, 2003.

Mayfield, Jeremy. Interview by NASCAR media tele-conference, June 8, 2004.

ADDRESSES

NASCAR
P.O. Box 2875
Daytona Beach, FL 32120
(386) 253-0611

Indianapolis Motor Speedway
4790 West 16th Street
Indianapolis, IN 46222

CRM Department
Guinness World Records Ltd.
8th Floor, 338 Euston Road
London, England NW1 3BD

Photo Credits:

AP/Wide World Photos: Cover, 8, 9, 10, 13, 15, 16, 18, 24, 26, 27, 29, 34, 35, 36, 46; © Hulton-Deutsch Collection/CORBIS: 14; © IMS Photo: 23, 30, 32, 41, 43, 45.

INTERNET SITES

www.nascar.com

This website is the best place to start learning more about NASCAR. It has the latest results and driver standings, but there are also pages where readers can learn more about the sport in general. The optional "Trackpass" service features archived video where footage of the Kurt Busch–Ricky Craven famous finish can be seen.

http://jayski.com

For readers interested in more in-depth NASCAR news, Jayski is the place to go. Every day, Jayski collects both facts and rumors from all over the country and puts it on the website. Many news items that happen in NASCAR appear somewhere on Jayski first.

http://indy500.com

The official site of the Indianapolis 500 is a comprehensive look back at the history of the race, as well as a glance toward the future. There are tons of facts and interesting tidbits to learn about the Indy 500.

www.guinnessworldrecords.com

See more about Andy Green's world land-speed record and read about many other world records on this site dedicated to bests and firsts. You can even find out how to make your own world record.

INDEX

ABOUT THE AUTHORS

Ann Graham Gaines received her graduate degrees in American Civilization and Library and Information Science from the University of Texas at Austin. Specializing in biographies and nonfiction, Gaines has been a freelance writer for 21 years. She lives by Gonzalez, Texas with her husband and their four children.

Jeff Gluck covers NASCAR, high schools, and the Atlantic Coast Conference for the *Rocky Mount Telegram* in North Carolina. A University of Delaware graduate, Gluck has also lived in California, Minnesota, and Colorado, visiting a total of 45 states along the way. Gluck has covered the Super Bowl, the Daytona 500, the ACC basketball tournament, and has attended three NCAA Final Fours.

Gluck and his wife, Jaime, reside in Rocky Mount, North Carolina.